BEASTQUEST®

AMULET OF AVANTIA

~← BOOK TWENTY-THREE ←~

BLAZE
THE ICE DRAGON

BEAST QUEST®

AMULET OF AVANTIA

-→ BOOK TWENTY-THREE ←-

BLAZE
THE ICE DRAGON

ADAM BLADE

ILLUSTRATED BY EZRA TUCKER

SCHOLASTIC INC.

New York Toronto London Auckland
Sydney Mexico City New Delhi Hong Kong

With special thanks to Michael Ford

For Alex McAteer

ISBN 978-0-545-27212-4

Beast Quest series created by Beast Quest Ltd., London.
BEAST QUEST is a trademark of Beast Quest Ltd.

Text © 2009 by Beast Quest Ltd. All rights reserved.
Cover illustration © 2009 by Steve Sims
Interior illustrations © 2012 by Scholastic Inc.

Published by Scholastic Inc., 557 Broadway, New York, NY 10012, by arrangement with Working Partners Ltd.
SCHOLASTIC and associated logos are trademarks and/or registered trademarks of Scholastic Inc.

12 11 10 9 8 7 6 5 4 3 2   12 13 14 15 16 17/0

Designed by Tim Hall
Printed in the U.S.A.   40
First printing, April 2012

BEAST QUEST

AMULET OF AVANTIA

#19: Nixa the Death Bringer

#20: Equinus the Spirit Horse

#21: Rashouk the Cave Troll

#22: Luna the Moon Wolf

#23: Blaze the Ice Dragon

#24: Stealth the Ghost Panther

BEASTQUEST

Character Guide

⇥ TOM ⇤

PREFERRED WEAPONS: Sword and magic shield

ALSO CARRIES: Destiny compass, jewel belt, and ghost map

SPECIAL SKILLS: Over the course of his Quest, Tom has gained many special items for his shield, giving him protection from fire, water, cold, and falling from heights, extra speed in battle, and magic healing ability. He also has the powers he gained from the golden armor, giving him incredible sight, courage, strength, endurance, sword skills, and energy.

⊷ Elenna ⊶

PREFERRED WEAPON: Bow & arrow

ALSO CARRIES: Nothing. Between her bow and her wolf, Silver, Elenna doesn't need anything else!

SPECIAL SKILLS: Not only is Elenna an expert hunter, she is also knowledgeable about boats and water. But most important, she can think quickly in tight spots, which has helped Tom more than once!

→ STORM ←

Tom's horse, a gift
from King Hugo.
Storm's good instincts
and speed have helped
Tom and Elenna from
the very beginning.

→ SILVER ←

Elenna's tame wolf and
constant companion. Not
only is Silver good to have
on their side in a fight,
but the wolf can also help
Tom and Elenna find
food when they're hungry.

⤙ ADURO ⤚

The good wizard of
Avantia and one of Tom's
closest allies. Aduro has
helped Tom many times,
but when Aduro was
captured by Malvel, Tom
was able to repay the
wizard by rescuing him.

⤙ MALVEL ⤚

Tom's enemy, determined
to enslave the Beasts of
Avantia and defeat Tom.
This evil wizard rules over
Gorgonia, the Dark
Realm. If he is near,
danger is sure to follow.

All hail, fellow followers of the Quest.

We have not met before but, like you, I have been watching Tom's adventures with a close eye. Do you know who I am? Have you heard of Taladon, the Master of the Beasts? I have returned — just in time for my son, Tom, to save me from a fate worse than death. The evil wizard, Malvel, has stolen something precious from me, and until Tom is able to complete another Quest, I cannot be returned to full life. I must wait between worlds, neither human nor ghost. I am half the man I once was and only Tom can return me to my former glory.

Will Tom have the strength of heart to help his father? Another Quest can test even the most determined hero. And there may be a heavy price for my son to pay if he defeats six more Beasts. . . .

All I can do is hope — that Tom is successful. Will you put your power behind Tom and wish him well? I know I can count on my son — can I count on you, too? Not a moment can be wasted. As this latest Quest unfolds, much rides on it. We must all be brave.

Taladon

CRIES OF PAIN DRIFTED FROM THE OPEN door of the hut, but Derlot hurried on past toward the herb garden. He was one of the lucky ones — the terrible sickness had spared him so far. When the first shepherd had fallen sick from a hyena bite, no one in Rokwin had dreamed that the disease would spread. Derlot had been away at the market in Stonewin for two days but by the time he returned the illness had touched almost every family in Rokwin. People were dying, and Derlot prayed that it was still in his power to help.

His father had been a medicine man, whose fame spread as far as the Plains. He'd claimed that one of his herbs, horn-fern, could cure any sickness in Avantia.

Derlot unlatched the gate to the herb garden and picked his way over the plants. Many of the herbs were withered and the weeds grew tall, but then he saw it — the horn-fern, its dark green leaves tipped with red.

Derlot stooped among the plants and took out his pruning knife. The blade was poised against the herb's stalk when a howling sound cut through the still summer air. Was it more hyenas?

Derlot stood up and looked around. Something was coiling through the trees toward him — a strange, dark shape, like the trailing smoke from a campfire. A sense of unease gripped him as he realized that it was moving too fast to be smoke.

Derlot felt his mouth drop open, as his eyes showed him something that his mind refused to accept. It was a dragon, but not one like those described in children's tales. Black and red scales covered the creature's snakelike body. His long tail swayed back and forth and appeared to propel the dragon through the air. The Beast opened his jaws and revealed icy blue fangs.

Derlot stumbled backward toward the open gate but tripped and landed on the path. The dragon hovered in the air above him, smoke coming from his nostrils, and opened his mouth. Derlot threw his hands up to protect himself — he knew what was coming.

Fire.

But suddenly a blast of freezing air enveloped him. He lowered his hands and saw that the garden had changed. The plants — including the precious horn-fern — were white with frost. The ground at his feet — even the laces of his boots — had frozen solid. The dragon had breathed ice.

The Beast hung lower in the sky, and Derlot was pinned by the dragon's gaze. There was something in the Beast's golden eyes — something almost human. Was this a Beast or a man? Or some terrible mixture of the two?

With a shriek, the dragon whipped his tail onto the ground. The earth shook with the impact and the plants shattered like glass.

The icy fragments became mist, blinding Derlot. As it cleared he saw the dragon flying toward the volcano in Stonewin.

Derlot surveyed the ruins of the garden and gave a low wail of despair. Without his herbs, the villagers in Rokwin were doomed.

And as for the people of Stonewin, they had their own terrors to face.

CHAPTER ONE

LEAVING THE FORBIDDEN LAND

THE SUN WAS JUST A SLIVER OVER THE HORIZON when Tom and Elenna left the Dark Wood. Tom was tired. The battle with Luna the Moon Wolf had tested him to the limit — and Elenna, too.

"Perhaps we should rest," suggested Elenna.

Tom glanced at his friend. Her knees were scuffed from where she'd stumbled and fallen earlier. He then looked at their brave animal companions. Silver, the wolf, trotted on ahead with his head low, and Tom's horse, Storm, staunchly plodded forward.

"I wish we could," Tom said regretfully. "But not yet."

He fingered the leather thong around his neck, where the pieces of the Amulet of Avantia hung. So far he'd retrieved four amulet parts and defeated each of the Ghost Beasts that had guarded them. But not until he had all six would his Quest be completed. Only *then* would he be able to bring his father, Taladon, back for good.

His next Quest, as his father had told him, was to defeat a dragon called Blaze.

"Well, we need to stop and check the map," said Elenna. "We can drink some water at the same time."

Tom nodded and sat down on a boulder. Elenna took their flask from Storm's saddlebag and drank, while Tom stretched out his hand in front of him.

"Map!" he commanded.

The air rippled as the ghostly map appeared in front of him. Without this gift from Aduro, they'd never have been able to find their way through the Forbidden Land or locate the Beasts.

A glowing line, like a thread of gold, snaked from where they stood at the edge of the Dark Wood, across the eastern fields, past a small village called Rokwin, and toward the town of Stonewin. It ended on the slopes of the volcano.

"Stonewin is where Epos lives," said Elenna, handing Tom the flask.

"I hope she's not in danger from this dragon," said Tom, taking a swig of water. Epos the Winged Flame was his loyal friend. Tom placed a hand over his eyes and gazed in the direction of Stonewin. His golden helmet, though kept in King Hugo's castle, gave him the power to see across great distances. He could see the volcano rising above the other mountains, but something was wrong.

"The crater isn't smoking," he told Elenna. "The volcano has smoked since the day I was born. Something is wrong."

"Then let's not waste any more time," Elenna insisted.

Now that Tom had seen their Quest set out on the ghost map, strength returned to his heart and they sped toward Avantian soil. As if sensing his urgency, Storm and Silver seemed to find new reserves of energy.

But even though his determination to complete his Quest was as hard as granite, another worry tugged at his mind. Each time Tom defeated one of Malvel's Ghost Beasts, a piece of his magical armor vanished, too. Now he had only two powers left.

Tom shook his head. The people of Stonewin, and maybe even Epos herself, needed him. He would not let them down. He would not let Malvel, the Dark Wizard, win.

Tom and Elenna reached the high wall that separated the Forbidden Land from Avantia. They passed silently through the unmanned gate.

"I'd forgotten that the sky could be so blue and the land so green," said Elenna.

Storm whinnied and wheeled about, bolting off across the lush grass. Silver spun in wild circles of joy.

"If we don't succeed in this Quest," said Tom, "Malvel's Beasts will take over Avantia, too — *everywhere* will be dead like the Forbidden Land."

"We won't let that happen," said Elenna.

A fork of lightning suddenly split the sky, which had rapidly darkened.

"The Forbidden Land may be behind you." Malvel's voice rumbled like thunder above their heads. "But the curse of the Ghost Beasts is still strong. Four you have faced, but the Beast to come will be your end. No mortal can defeat the dragon's breath."

"I do not fear Blaze!" shouted Tom.

Malvel laughed again. "Blaze will not be your only enemy this time. You will face two adversaries as one."

The storm ended as quickly as it had begun and Malvel was gone.

"Two adversaries!" said Elenna. "What does he mean?"

"I don't know," said Tom grimly. "But I'm not afraid to find out."

↦ CHAPTER TWO ↤

A LAND OF ICE

TOM AND ELENNA MOUNTED STORM AND galloped across the plain while Silver streaked beside them. Soon they were deep in Avantian territory, making good progress toward Stonewin.

Tom scanned the road ahead for danger, but to his surprise they saw no one at all. There weren't even any sheep grazing on the plains. Tom slowed Storm to a canter and, once they were on the grass, vaulted off the horse and crouched to inspect the ground.

"There's frost on this grass!"

Elenna frowned. "But it's *summer*."

Tom shrugged and mounted his horse again, before they continued their journey, passing lush green fields and bushes heavy with berries. A short while later, they came to a pond and Tom guided Storm and Silver over to the water to have a well-earned drink. But as they approached the edge, he saw that the surface was frozen over.

"This is no ordinary cold weather, Elenna," he said. "Some places are green and alive, while a few paces away the ground is frozen solid." Using the base of his shield, Tom smashed a hole in the ice so that Storm and Silver could drink.

"How can that be?" said Elenna. "Stonewin's volcano has always made the surrounding areas warmer than usual, not colder."

They raced on. Soon, though, they came to a path that was covered with a great swathe of ice.

"We'll have to go slower," he told Elenna. "We can't risk injuring Storm on the slippery ground."

Picking their way carefully down the path, they passed a copse of trees bejeweled with frost and saw stone walls covered with ice.

Soon they came upon a signpost. One arm pointed toward Errinel, Tom's village, and the other to Rokwin, which he knew was on the way to Stonewin.

"Let's hope we can find someone to tell us what's going on," said Tom.

But he soon saw that the road toward Rokwin was deserted as well.

"People should be trading along this route," said Elenna. "Where is everyone?" Tom shared her bemusement. Even in the worst of weather the people of Avantia went about their business.

Up ahead, Tom heard a noise. Something was approaching from around the bend in the road. Tom's hand fell to his sword hilt. Wild animals roamed Avantia, and he wouldn't be caught off guard. His friend, who sat behind him, had already unhooked her bow.

"Ready?" she asked, nocking an arrow.

Tom nodded and held Storm's reins a bit tighter.

A mare trotted around the corner and her rider, who lay close against her back, steered her.

Tom breathed a sigh of relief and he let go of his sword. "Stop there! I need to talk to you."

But the horse didn't slow.

"Stop. Please!" Tom guided Storm to stand sideways across the path.

The horse drew up in front of them. The rider was slumped in the saddle and only now turned his head slowly toward them. Tom recoiled when he saw the scabs covering the man's face.

Silver let out a whine of unease.

"Are you all right?" Elenna asked the man.

"Go back," the sick man whispered. "Rokwin is doomed."

With those words, his eyes closed and he slipped from the saddle like a sack of grain. Tom could see that he was dead before he hit the ground. Silver took a few nervous steps toward the body, while Elenna got ready to dismount.

"No!" said Tom, guiding Storm between the man and the wolf.

"What's wrong?" said Elenna.

"I think this man died of an infection," Tom replied. "We mustn't touch him."

Tom steered along the edge of the path, as far as the bend in the road. There he dismounted and used his magical sight to look into the town of Rokwin. No smoke issued from the chimneys of the low houses, and no one walked the streets.

A flash of movement caught his eye. Behind a large storehouse, a crowd of townspeople were gathered. But something was wrong. They walked in aimless circles, bumping into one another and falling over. Their faces were like the dead rider's —

pale, with oozing sores. Some awful disease had infected the whole village.

With a troubled heart, Tom walked back to Elenna.

"What did you see?" she asked.

He told her the fate of the unfortunate villagers and she gasped. "What can we do for them?"

"First, we have to find out what caused this horror," said Tom.

And make sure the same thing doesn't happen to us, he thought to himself. His current Quest had just become twice as dangerous.

CHAPTER THREE

AMBUSHED

"PERHAPS I CAN HELP THEM," SAID ELENNA. "My aunt taught me how to use herbs as medicine."

Tom shook his head. "You can't, Elenna. You might become infected, too."

"I can't just leave them, Tom," she replied hotly. "What about Epos's feather?"

Tom looked at the golden feather embedded in his shield, a reminder of his last Quest to Stonewin, when he freed Epos the Winged Flame. The feather's healing powers had helped him many times, but this was different.

"The feather works on cuts and bruises," he

explained. "The emerald I took from Skor in Gorgonia heals broken bones. . . . But this is an illness . . . a *disease.* There's nothing we can do. We must focus on our Quest and hope there's time to help afterward."

Tom saw Elenna clench her fist with frustration. He put a hand on her shoulder and she ducked her head sadly.

"Is there another route to Stonewin?" she asked after a moment, her voice hoarse.

Tom summoned his map again, and studied its shimmering surface.

"We can skirt the lower reaches of Rokwin, instead of going directly through it," he said, pointing to a thin line on the map. "Behind the forest there."

They set off on their new route and found that this way was deserted as well. Soon Rokwin dipped out of sight behind a bank of tall trees. Elenna was quiet as they rode and Tom could tell that, like him, she felt guilty at leaving the suffering villagers behind.

The road gradually became rougher, the ground covered in loose rocks and hidden dips. Silver scouted the way, nose to the ground, and guided them onward, but the wolf stopped as he came to a fallen tree that blocked the path.

Tom halted his horse.

"The locals must have been cutting down trees for timber," said Elenna. "The illness meant that they had to stop."

"Or they blocked the road on purpose," said Tom.

The trunk was as wide as he was tall. Skirting the fallen tree would be almost impossible, as the path was narrow and the land bordering them on either side was sheer and rocky.

"We'll have to turn back," said Elenna.

"We can't," Tom replied. "There's no other way

to Stonewin." He patted Storm's neck. "What do you think, boy? Think you can clear that trunk?"

Storm tossed his mane, and stamped his front hooves. Tom knew he could rely on his horse's bravery every time.

"Hold on tight," he said to Elenna, and she gripped his waist.

Tom dug his heels into Storm's flank and the stallion bolted forward, hooves scattering rocks everywhere. As the fallen trunk loomed, Tom lifted the reins and gripped Storm's sides with his knees. Suddenly, they were airborne and he felt his weight slam back in the saddle.

Storm's hooves cleared the bark by a finger's breadth, landing with a jolt on the other side. "Well done!" cried Tom, slapping his horse's neck. He looked back and saw Silver scramble over, and stand on top of the trunk, panting.

"Catch your breath, boy," Tom called to the wolf. "You deserve —"

Something whizzed past Tom's ear, fast and hot, and he saw Silver spring away from the trunk and into the trees ahead.

"Take cover!" shouted Elenna.

Tom dragged Storm's reins around, as a flare of light appeared between the trees ahead.

A flaming arrow.

The blazing shaft shot from the cover of the forest. Without a thought, Tom raised his shield-arm in defense. The arrow buried itself in his shield with a thud.

Suddenly, dozens of orange pricks of light were visible in the forest, all illuminating angry faces.

Elenna sprung off of Storm, and Tom vaulted out of the saddle as well. He hit Storm's rear with his shield. "Go!" he shouted.

Storm bolted into the trees just as a hail of flaming arrows descended. Tom dragged Elenna behind him and threw up his shield, hearing the arrows slam into it.

The volley ended, and someone shouted, "Fire again!"

Tom held up one hand, showing them he was not a threat. "We mean you no harm!" he shouted out. "We're on a mission of peace."

Some muttering followed; then a voice called back, "Then turn around and go. You're not welcome here."

"We must get to Stonewin," Tom said. "The main road is filled with sickness."

"There's no sickness here, boy. We mean for it to stay that way."

Tom suddenly understood their anger and took a risk in lowering his shield. A row of desperate faces looked back.

"This is our only option," said Tom. "Please . . . let us through. We're not sick."

One of the men stepped out of the trees, his bow lowered but the string taut with a loaded arrow. "Come forward, then," he said. "Both of you."

Tom and Elenna took a few steps, side by side, drawing within ten paces of the group. Tom felt his confidence returning. Now that he wasn't being shot at, he could reason with these people. Show them that he wasn't a threat.

The ground beneath him suddenly seemed to rise up, and Tom and Elenna were lifted off their feet and pulled up into the air. They were caught in some sort of net that hung from a tree.

It was a trap.

Beside him Elenna gave a scream of rage and fear and began to lash out at the net. Tom's eyes focused on the man below, who pointed his arrow straight up at them.

This time there was no escape.

CHAPTER FOUR

A VILLAGE IN NEED

THE BOWMAN'S HAND — POISED TO RELEASE the bowstring — shook with nerves.

Tom struggled to right himself in the net, but his legs kept on slipping through the gaps.

"Don't shoot," Tom implored. "Look at us — we're not sick."

"We can't risk it," said a voice from the woods. "Kill them."

"Very well," said the archer, holding the bow firmer now.

A scuffling sound came from the trees. Tom saw the man's eyes drop to his right and his lips part in surprise. Silver suddenly leaped from the shadows and sank his teeth into the man's arm. The archer screamed and dropped the bow and arrow.

Their enemy now distracted, Tom managed to draw his sword and hacked at the net.

"Hold on to me," he shouted to Elenna, and he felt her grip his waist. As the net fell open, he clutched a rope with one hand and they swung out toward the archers who were still among the trees. Tom let go and they dropped onto their enemies.

Elenna was up in a flash, her hunting dagger at the throat of an elderly man. Tom rolled across the ground, and pointed his sword at the chest of the injured archer.

Silver came to stand at Tom's side.

"Lower your bows!" shouted Elenna, pressing the point of her knife against the elderly man's skin. Tom knew his friend would never harm an Avantian, but she was playing the role very well.

He got to his feet, keeping the injured archer at the end of his sword. One by one, the flaming arrow points were extinguished.

"Don't hurt him," said the elderly man. "He's only frightened, like the rest of us."

"We won't hurt anybody," said Tom. "I only want to talk."

Elenna released the man, who warily hobbled forward to Tom. His eyes were dark with lack of sleep and his skin gray like old parchment.

"My name is Derlot," he said. "And I come from the village of Rokwin."

"I know the place," said Tom.

Derlot's face clouded. "You wouldn't recognize it now. Disease has ravaged it." He waved his hand at the faces between the trees. "We're the only ones who escaped."

The *clop-clop* of Storm's hooves made Tom turn. His stallion came out of the shelter of the trees and walked to his side.

"Where are you and your companions heading?" asked Derlot.

"Stonewin," said Tom, cautiously. "We are trying to reach the volcano there."

Derlot's eyes widened, and he lowered his voice. "If the volcano is your destination, you must know of another threat to Avantia."

"What do you mean?" Tom asked.

Derlot stepped closer. "The plague is not the only curse to afflict this land. There's a dragon, too!"

Elenna looked at Tom in surprise, but Tom kept his face expressionless. The good wizard Aduro had told him to never, ever reveal the truth of his Quests to anyone.

"A dragon!" he said. "Do they really exist?"

"I saw it with my own eyes," said Derlot. "A dragon that breathes ice instead of fire. My herbs to cure the ill were destroyed because of him."

Elenna and Tom shared a look. Did this explain the frozen ponds and icicles on the trees? Was Blaze responsible?

"If you don't believe me," said Derlot, "I can show you my herb garden. I just hope the dragon doesn't return."

"Let's go," said Tom.

Derlot led the way through the dense forest. Tom pulled Storm by his reins and Elenna came behind with Silver at her side.

"No one in the village believes me," said Derlot, stooping under a branch. "But I know what I saw."

As they penetrated deeper among the trees, slowly climbing the lower slopes of Rokwin, Tom noticed the air becoming colder.

Storm snorted and air formed white clouds at his nostrils. Tom could see his own breath, too. They'd been traveling for some time, and Tom wondered if the old man was lost.

"Not far now," whispered Derlot, pulling his cloak more tightly around him.

They emerged into a clearing and Elenna gasped. Tom saw that the ground was white with frost, and crystals of ice glittered like tiny diamonds on the tips of broken stalks and ruined shrubs.

"This was the herb garden," said Derlot, "and my only hope of curing the sickness that afflicts my people."

"Poor thing!" Elenna pointed to a rabbit among the encrusted plants. It was frozen mid-jump, its ears sticking up and its body stretched out as it had tried to flee. This was more than just unseasonably cold weather.

Silver sniffed at the frozen rabbit, and then

turned his head to Elenna, as if confused that his prey was not running away.

"Do you believe me now?" asked Derlot. "About the dragon?"

Tom nodded, feeling a chill in his heart that had nothing to do with the freezing cold air. "I believe you," he said.

This time Malvel and his Beasts had gone too far.

CHAPTER FIVE

THE HYENAS OF ROKWIN

As THEY LEFT THE COLD CLEARING BEHIND, Elenna fell in beside Derlot. "How was the sickness caused?" she asked.

"Five days ago," Derlot said, "one of the shepherds, Adam, was attacked and bitten by a hyena in the dark. He only managed to escape by beating the animal off with his staff and then climbing a tree."

Elenna held out her arm to help Derlot across a narrow stream.

"A hyena?" asked Tom.

"Yes," Derlot continued. "It was strange because they don't normally come so close to Rokwin."

The old man sighed. "Adam became sick in the night, sweating and mumbling in his sleep. By the next morning, the nurse looking after him was beginning to show signs of the same illness."

"It was spreading," said Tom, guiding Storm among a collection of boulders.

Derlot nodded. "The following dusk brought more hyenas. A dozen of them made a home in the thickets on the south side of the village. Their howls kept everyone awake, and we posted archers and slingers around Rokwin's fences, but under the full moon they attacked." Derlot shook his head mournfully. "They snuck into houses and bit whomever they could find."

"Did they kill many?" asked Elenna.

"That's the strange thing," said Derlot. "It was almost as though these hyenas didn't come to kill. They would bite only once, and then slip away back to their den in the thickets. By the morning, half of the village was ill. Those who weren't decided to flee. . . ."

This sounds like Malvel's magic, Tom thought. Were these hyenas the second adversary the Dark Wizard had spoken of?

When they reached the path again, it was almost dusk and the other villagers were waiting.

Elenna took Tom aside, while Derlot went to talk with his followers.

"Tom, we have to help these people," she whispered. "Even if it means delaying the Quest."

"You're right," he said. "I think Malvel is behind this, and we have to fight him wherever he appears. But what can we do about this plague?"

Elenna frowned for a moment, and then her face lit up. "My aunt always taught me that powdered willow bark was good for animal bites. Perhaps it'll work here, too."

"Do you have any?" Tom asked.

Elenna shook her head. "But the villagers may know where to find some."

She turned to the frightened group and asked them if any willow trees grew nearby.

"Down by the river," replied a stout young woman. "It's a fair walk, but the trees are plentiful."

As Elenna gathered the villagers to head to the riverbank, Tom jumped onto Storm.

"Where are you going?" asked Derlot.

"To deal with the hyenas," said Tom. "On the south side of the village, you say?"

"Yes," said Derlot, "but there are many. A boy like you will be torn to pieces."

Tom smiled. "I've faced hyenas before. They don't frighten me."

Elenna was ready to go. "Be careful," Tom warned her. "There may be hyenas by the river, too."

Elenna crouched beside Silver and stroked the thick hair behind his neck. "I have Silver to look after me. He's not scared of a few mangy hyenas — are you?"

Silver growled and bared his teeth. Tom felt much better knowing the wolf was at his friend's side.

He spurred Storm into action and galloped off along the road toward Rokwin.

Night was falling and every sound was magnified in Tom's ears. The forest on either side seemed to press down upon him. Owls seemed to hoot in welcome as he passed the outskirts of the village of Rokwin.

Soon the road disappeared and Tom found himself surrounded by thorny bushes. *This must be the thicket that Derlot talked of*, he thought. Storm slowed, tossing his head with a whinny. Tom stroked the horse's mane and slipped off his back. There were tracks on the ground, large paw prints — hyenas.

A low growling from within the thicket reached his ears.

"Stay here," he whispered to Storm, and set off in a crouch, following the sound. The belly laugh of hyenas drifted over the night air as Tom creeped between the sharp, thorny branches. Then he saw them.

A pack of mangy creatures, their ribs showing through their hides, were in a clearing fighting. Grass and dust flew up as they tore at one another with teeth and claws. Saliva drooled from their jaws and they howled and gnashed their teeth. Tom counted them: ten in all. He would have to form a plan to deal with so many at once.

Tom felt his nose twitch. A rank smell, like rotten meat, had filled his nostrils. Then he heard a tiny shuffle nearby. Tom twisted, drawing his sword just in time as a snarling hyena leaped from behind him. He thrust his sword toward the animal and it died on his blade. With his foot, Tom pushed the dead creature off his weapon.

The growls from the clearing had stopped. Tom looked back.

Ten pairs of eyes were on him, like twenty silver coins sparkling in the moonlight. One by one, the hyenas loped forward.

Then they broke into a run, coming straight for Tom.

There was death in their eyes.

→ CHAPTER SIX ←

A NIGHT ATTACK

TOM KNEW HE COULDN'T FACE THEM ALL AT once and sprinted back toward Storm. He no longer had his ability to jump great distances, so he threw himself onto Storm's back and scrambled into the saddle. The hyenas surrounded him.

"Go!" he yelled, kicking his stallion's sides. Storm charged straight through the hyenas, causing them to scatter. One was trampled beneath the stallion's hooves and yelped out.

The other hyenas regrouped and howled into the night, flashing their long yellow fangs.

A plan formed in Tom's head, but he'd have to make the hyenas follow him for it to work. Storm reared on his hind legs in alarm as the scavenging creatures came closer, but Tom calmed him down.

"It's all right, boy," he said. "We're going to get out of this."

The hyenas paced back and forth, arching their spines, the hair on their necks standing straight up.

Again, he rode Storm directly at the mangy creatures. One leaped up, but Tom swiped at it with the flat of his sword. The others dodged aside, thin black lips curled in snarls.

Tom galloped back along the road, past Rokwin and through the forest.

Behind him, he could hear the yapping jaws of the hyenas as they pursued. They were close. Storm charged between the trees fearlessly, the branches whipping at Tom's face.

A bank of solid trunks blocked the path and Tom changed direction. Two hyenas moved quickly through the underbrush and threw themselves at Storm's flank. Tom took his hands from the reins and beat one away with his shield, stabbing at the other.

Storm burst through the far side of the forest. They were out in the fields again, heading back toward the Forbidden Land. Sweat soaked Storm's hair and his mane streamed in the darkness, but he galloped on. When it seemed they were pulling away, Tom slowed the mount to keep their pursuers in the chase. He couldn't afford to lose them now. Not when his plan was nearly complete.

They passed the frozen pond where he and Elenna had reentered Avantia and then plunged back into the Dark Wood.

From his last Quest, Tom recalled and used the complicated paths that led between the trees of Luna the Moon Wolf's home. It was as if they'd been etched into his brain. The yellow jewel he won defeating Narga the Sea Monster gave him a perfect memory. He threaded between the bare silvered trunks. The padding of the hyenas' paws grew softer. Tom risked a look behind, and saw only a four or five of the animals slinking through the shadows. They looked uncertain. His ruse had worked. They were disoriented now and in unfamiliar land. And several of the hyenas had already gotten lost in the forest.

Tom's legs ached from gripping Storm's flanks, but he did not slacken his grip. He crisscrossed the woods, until the last of the hyenas fell to the ground, its tongue lolling from its exhausted mouth. Then Tom galloped away, leaving it deep in the maze of the dark trees. With any luck, none of the hyenas would return to spread their illness ever again.

It was the middle of the night when Tom trotted back down the forest path toward Rokwin. Gray smoke curled into the sky from the small fires that lit the outskirts of the village. The uninfected villagers whom he'd seen in the forest were huddled at the firesides, boiling a foul-smelling broth in iron pots. Tom found Elenna beside one. Silver lay patiently at her feet.

"You're back!" she said.

Tom slipped from Storm's back. "The hyenas will no longer be a problem."

"We've been busy here as well. We found the willow bark," Elenna said, and they walked to where two thin and bedraggled women were sleeping soundly. Another was sitting up, sipping from a wooden cup.

"These women were all sick not long ago."

Tom smiled through his weariness.

"Your friend is very skilled," said a voice he recognized. Tom saw Derlot coming toward them. "We've enough medicine to heal everyone. Soon all of Rokwin will be cured."

Tom was happy, but he couldn't allow himself to relax. One obstacle was overcome, but Malvel's Beast still awaited them.

"We should go," he said.

"No!" exclaimed Derlot. "We must give you a feast. The both of you have saved our lives."

"I'm afraid that we have another problem to deal with," said Tom. "And it cannot wait."

"The dragon?" Derlot whispered.

Tom nodded, unable to lie. He climbed onto Storm, and helped Elenna up behind him. "Goodbye, Derlot," he said.

"Farewell, young heroes," the old man replied.

The villagers cheered and waved them off, shouting their thanks. Storm galloped along the rocky path toward Stonewin, Silver at his side, and soon the crackle of the fires and the smell of wood smoke were far behind.

Tom felt as though he was returning home when he saw the volcano rise up ahead in the distance. He smiled as he remembered the last time he had visited this place — his Quest to free Epos. At first, the sight of the gigantic winged flame with her blazing feathers had filled him with dread. Little did he know then that, once rescued from Malvel's spell, Epos would become one of his most loyal friends. But the volcano had lost its bitter smell of sulfur, and the air wasn't warm as it should be. He frowned. It was as if the great volcano had become dormant, and sapped of life.

Using his magical sight, Tom scoured the slopes for Malvel's fifth Ghost Beast. Nothing stirred in the darkness. "We should stop for the night," he said. "We can look for Blaze when the sun rises."

Elenna seemed happy to rest, and lay with Silver in the shelter of a large boulder. Storm lounged by the side of the path and Tom sat against his soft underbelly, determined to keep his eyes open in case danger approached.

His mind returned to Epos. Was the winged flame in danger? If Malvel had harmed her, Tom vowed that his revenge would be swift. But his anger couldn't keep him awake. The stars began to drift in front of his eyes, and he felt sleep envelop him.

He woke with a start. An icy feeling choked his chest.

Tom looked down and saw something moving across his torso. His hands touched the black and red scales, thick as saddle leather, which coiled around him.

Blaze!

CHAPTER SEVEN

AT THE CRATER'S EDGE

PANIC AND PAIN CHOKED TOM'S THROAT AS THE dragon's length tightened around him. He tried to stand up, but he couldn't move his legs. The dragon had looped his snaky form around Tom's lower body, too. A pair of gleaming eyes set in a narrow head on a long neck swung around to look straight at him.

Tom stared as a forked tongue, black as night, flickered in and out between the Beast's bloodless reptilian lips. The dragon brought his head right up to Tom's face. Tom wanted to look away, but he couldn't. There was something about the dragon's eyes. They weren't like any Beast's he'd seen before. They looked . . . human.

And Tom was sure he'd seen them somewhere before. He tried to call out to Elenna, but a thin wheezing sound was the only noise that came out of his mouth. He writhed, fighting to free his arms. He twisted his shoulders and jerked his hips, anything to loosen the dragon's death hold. As if in response, the scaly body contracted and Tom felt his ribs begin to crack.

Storm snorted in the darkness and Elenna slept on a few paces away, oblivious to the danger. Tom had to wake her. If he died, she would be next. He saw his shield leaning up against a rock. If he could knock it over, the sound might awaken Elenna.

As the Beast's muscular grip shifted again, Tom gasped once more as he tried to draw breath. The ice dragon's head didn't move — it was as if Blaze wanted to *watch* him suffocate. Then Tom realized where he had seen those eyes before.

Malvel!

Somehow the Dark Wizard was *inside* this Beast, controlling him with his evil magic.

Tom stretched his leg toward the shield and managed to slip his foot behind it. With the last vestiges of his strength, he flicked the shield up into the air and it clattered onto a small rock.

Elenna was on her feet in a heartbeat.

Tom's vision darkened and his limbs grew weak. Was this the end?

Suddenly, the death grip weakened and air filled Tom's lungs. He immediately saw the cause. One of Elenna's arrows was sticking out from Blaze's body. Silver charged forward and tried to bite the dragon's side, but his teeth slid helplessly off the thick scales.

"Hold on!" Elenna shouted, stringing another

arrow. Tom wriggled free and rolled across the ground toward his sword. But before he could grab the hilt, the tentacle-like coil of Blaze's tail wrapped around his ankle. Tom looked over his shoulder and saw that he was being dragged back toward the Beast's gaping jaws. The dragon's teeth were icy blue, but his mouth was red like blood.

Tom pulled himself by his fingernails toward the sword, feeling his sinews stretch to their limit. He locked his fingers around the hilt. As he was pulled backward, he turned and swiped at the Beast's head. But the blade passed straight through the Beast and thwacked into the ground. Blaze's body was now see-through. He'd turned into a ghost!

Tom felt a swell of rage in his chest as he got to his feet. Like the other Beasts on this Quest, Blaze had the ability to transform from a real to a ghostly form in an instant. Tom swung again, trying to hack at the semitransparent scales, but

his sword met no resistance and passed through the Beast once more. The color rushed back into Blaze's body as the Beast took on his flesh-and-blood form.

"Look!" shouted Elenna, pointing. "The amulet piece!"

Tom's heart thumped as he saw that the amulet fragment was lodged between the scales where Blaze's body met his head. Tom hopped onto a boulder, and leaped toward the dragon as it reached for his prize.

The Beast lashed his tail out like a whip and Tom was struck in the chest and fell to the ground. He watched helplessly as the ice dragon took to the skies, climbing steadily through the air, his tail whipping out behind him and thrusting him upward. Silver howled at the departing Beast, while Storm neighed angrily.

Blaze hovered above the volcano's crater and Malvel's laughter boomed, shaking the slopes.

"Come and catch me . . . if you dare." With those words, Blaze dipped his head and plunged into the heart of the crater.

Tom got to his feet.

"It sounds like a trap," said Elenna.

The first pale light of dawn was breaking. Tom realized they hadn't slept long, but he was not tired. Coming so close to death had made him feel more alive than ever.

"We've outsmarted Malvel before. . . . We'll outsmart him again! We must go after Blaze."

Tom saw Storm's legs twitch, as if the horse was eager to start the day.

"You stay here, boy," said Tom. "We're better on foot on the volcano."

Elenna stroked Silver. "And you look after him," she said.

Waving good-bye to their animal companions, Tom and Elenna took off up the path. The cold air cut right through them.

"Do you remember the last time we were here?" asked Elenna as they climbed up the craggy rock face. "Lava flowed down from the crater edge."

Tom stopped, helping Elenna up onto a ledge. "The villagers would have lost their homes but we succeeded in our Quest and saved Epos."

"Epos . . ." said Elenna, voice grave. "Where is she? Why is it so cold up here?"

Tom looked up toward the crater, where Epos made her nest. So far he hadn't even felt her presence. His anger tightened like a knot inside him. "If Malvel has harmed my friend," he said, "he will pay."

→ Chapter Eight ←

Epos Imprisoned

THE AIR GREW EVEN COLDER AS THEY CLIMBED up the winding path of the barren slopes. It was as though all the laws of nature had been turned upside down.

As they headed toward the crater's edge, the wind sounded like a thousand screams as it carried Tom's breath away on icy currents.

He looked over at Elenna, noticing that her lips had started to turn purple. "Are you all right to go on?" he shouted above the wind.

"W-w-while I c-c-c-can still fire an arrow, I won't stop," she called back.

Pain throbbed in his aching legs as Tom finally picked his way over the final yards to the lip of the volcano's crater. Long ago he'd watched Epos rise from this very spot, majestic with her ruby red feathers aflame and talons dipped in gold. Where was she now?

Elenna reached his side, the wind lashing her hair across her pale face. They both peered into the chasm below.

Tom's heart filled with despair. The shallow sides of the crater were covered in crystals of ice. Great blue-white columns rose up from the depths like towers of diamonds. Blaze was nowhere to be seen.

The lava pool itself, which should have been bubbling at the bottom of the crater, was totally frozen over with a sheet of solid ice. And there, below the surface, was a sight that made Tom's blood run colder still. Epos, her mighty wings spread wide, was trapped under the ice shelf!

"Poor Epos!" gasped Elenna. "Only Malvel could be so cruel."

Tom was almost speechless with anger. "We have to rescue her."

They began to climb down the steep walls of the crater, placing each foot with care. Epos glided up to the roof of her frozen prison. A fireball formed between her talons like a miniature sun, and she hurled it against the ice shelf.

"She's trying to escape," said Elenna.

Epos did the same again, and this time Tom saw a crack appear in the frozen sheet of lava. They reached the flatter ground near the frozen lava pool and watched as another one of the winged flame's fiery orbs hit the ice and caused another fissure to appear in the ice shelf.

"It's working," said Elenna.

"One more, Epos!" Tom urged. "You can do it!"

As the fourth fireball was growing between the winged flame's talons, a roar from above rattled the walls of the volcano. Tom looked up. Blaze was diving toward them, mouth open wide, razor teeth dripping with drool and his human eyes glinting with ferocious intent. Malvel's cackle echoed off the crater walls.

The Beast swooped past them, a surge of air blasting from his mouth, which he spread over the ice shelf. Tom felt his heart sink — the frozen sheet had grown to twice as thick now.

Epos's globes of fire were having little effect on the toughened barrier, but still she tried, hurling ball after ball of flame against the ice. Each time it looked like her efforts might pay off, the Beast blew more freezing air onto the ice. Blaze seemed interested only in keeping Epos imprisoned, and paid no attention to Tom and Elenna.

"There must be a way to stop Blaze," said Elenna.

"We don't have to stop him," said Tom. "We just have to keep him busy and give Epos a chance to escape. Can you distract him long enough for me to get down to the ice shelf?"

Elenna had an arrow strung before the words were out of his mouth.

"Good," he said. "Get Blaze's attention."

Elenna loosed an arrow across the cavern at the dragon and Blaze shrieked in pain as the arrow found its mark in his side. Tom began scrambling down to the ice, sliding over the slippery ground. He saw Elenna fire another arrow, but this time Blaze shifted into his ghost form and it passed straight through him.

Tom was now down on the ice. Seeing him so close, Epos keened, hurling another fireball at the shelf.

"Look out!" Tom heard Elenna call. He turned to see Blaze flying right at him. He dove aside, as a blast of ice shot from the dragon's mouth. Tom sprang up and lunged at the Beast. He swung his sword out at Blaze as the dragon wheeled in the air, but at the last instant the Beast became a ghost and the blade passed through him. With another freezing blast of air, Blaze restored the ice shelf.

How can I defeat this dragon? Tom wondered. *I can't even get near him.*

Undaunted, Epos lit another fiery orb, the bright light shining through the ice, casting Tom's shadow on the volcano's wall. Tom saw Blaze coming at him again, and he sprung up and tried to drive the point of his sword into the Beast's heart. Once more, Blaze evaporated into ghostly form and the attack was in vain. The evil Beast hovered, transparent, just above Tom's head.

"Out of tricks?" Malvel's voice bellowed.

Tom's anger took over, and he slashed wildly at the air.

Out of the corner of his eye, Tom saw his shadow make the same movement, and to his surprise Blaze shrieked and writhed. It was as though Tom's

shadow's blade had somehow connected with the Ghost Beast. A fat drop of blue blood dripped from the Beast's scales.

Tom's eyes were drawn to Epos. For some reason the winged flame was clutching a fireball, but hadn't thrown it. The light from the fireball meant that Tom cast a looming shadow on the wall. Could it be . . . ? Yes, Epos was telling him something very important.

Tom stabbed wildly again, and his shadow's blade connected with the Ghost Beast once more and Blaze roared in pain a second time, his glinting eyes showing confusion. But Tom was not confused — he now understood why Epos was holding the fireball. It made Tom's shadow permanent. Tom's skin tingled as he realized what this meant.

I might not be able to fight the Ghost Beast, but my shadow can!

Chapter Nine

Shadow Warrior

Tom readied himself to strike again, but
the Ghost Beast surged upward, landing on an icy
ledge where Tom's shadow sword couldn't reach
him. Tom knew that he had to press his advantage
while the Beast was stunned with his injuries, but
how could he attack Blaze with his shadow while
the Ghost Beast cowered out of range?

But of course — *the white diamond!*

Tom checked his belt, where the jewel was
lodged. He'd won it from Kaymon the Gorgon
Hound.

The diamond gave him the power to separate
himself from his shadow. He climbed up to Elenna,

who had trained her arrow on the ice dragon, just in case he shifted out of his ghostly form. He whispered in her ear, so that Malvel wouldn't be able to hear his plan.

"My shadow is the only thing that can harm Blaze while he is in his ghost form," he said. "And the only way my shadow can reach him is if I use the jewel from Kaymon."

Elenna frowned. "It's too dangerous, Tom," she whispered back. "When your shadow is separated from you, your body can't move. You won't be able to defend yourself if Blaze comes after you."

Tom could see that she spoke out of worry for him, but he would not be swayed. "I know it's a risk," he said. "But if we wait here, Blaze will recover and he'll freeze us just like the hare in Derlot's garden."

Suddenly, the winged flame gave a tired-sounding cry and the fireball in her talons faded a bit. Tom looked back at Elenna, whose face had hardened.

"I'll do my best to protect you," Elenna said. "If Blaze comes too close, I'll have my arrows ready."

Tom gave Elenna a quick hug of thanks, then took a deep breath, calling on the power of the white diamond.

Dizziness gripped his head, and he put out a foot to steady himself before he opened his eyes.

But he hadn't moved.

"Tom," said Elenna's voice. "It's working!"

The leg of his shadow had peeled away. Tom ordered the other leg to do the same.

The shadow obeyed. Soon, it was standing beside him as though it were a whole other person. In his mind, Tom told it to unsheathe its sword. Though his own arms were still as a statue, Shadow Tom drew his blade.

Do battle with Blaze, he told his shadow. Tom was powerless to move, but the shadow did exactly as he asked, darting across the ice and clambering up the far side of the cavern wall toward the ledge where Blaze was beginning to stir once again.

Quicker! Tom urged. His shadow rippled silently over the wall, and heaved itself up.

Shadow Tom leaped onto the ledge, and the Ghost Beast turned to face him, striking out with his tail. The shadow ducked and countered with his blade, bringing out a curdling cry of agony from the ice dragon. Blaze leaped off the ledge and glided downward, blowing another fresh layer of ice onto Epos's prison. Tom's shadow jumped down, too, sword held aloft, chasing Blaze relentlessly.

Why didn't Malvel's Beast stay and fight? Tom wondered. *Why is it so important to keep the ice shelf in place?*

Epos, looking reenergized, lit another fireball, while Blaze and Shadow Tom faced off again. The Ghost Beast darted forward, but dodged Shadow Tom's sword at the last moment, then flicked his muscular tail out. It struck Tom's shadow in the head, and knocked him back against the wall. Tom felt the bruising pain as though it were his own.

But instead of going after Shadow Tom, Blaze breathed another icy blast at Epos, refreezing the ice shelf.

Realization dawned in Tom's mind. Blaze was an *ice dragon*. Epos was a *winged flame*. Just as ice could imprison Epos, what if *heat* was Blaze's enemy? Was that why Epos was imprisoned?

Tom wished he could tell Elenna his theory. She might be able to help Epos break the ice and escape. But his voice, like the rest of him, was paralyzed. No, he would have to handle this on his own.

Somehow, he would have to *move*.

His brain told him it was impossible, but his heart told him otherwise.

Tom sent his shadow running to the far side of the cavern, and Blaze followed. While they were busy, Tom channeled all his willpower into making his frozen limbs move. He felt a sweat break out all over his body, and his heart thundered in his chest. He managed to make his head turn, but it felt as though the sinews in his neck were being torn apart. Next he concentrated on moving his arm. It was like trying to lift an anvil in the blacksmith's forge. His body screamed with pain, but the arm finally moved a fraction. His eyes caught Elenna's expression, her mouth wide-open in amazement.

It took all his strength of heart but Tom dragged his body over to Epos's ice prison and he lifted his shield above his head. Beneath the ice, Epos flapped her wings madly in anticipation. The sight was enough to drive Tom on. With a growl of determination, Tom brought the shield down, ramming it into the ice.

A crack splintered the center of the sheet and Tom fell to his knees. He watched with delight as Epos burst free in a shower of icy splinters and

took to the air. The crater was suddenly filled with golden light, and all around, the ice began to melt and trickle in rivulets down the walls.

Malvel's cry of despair split the cavern, and Blaze's ghostly form suddenly became solid once again. Through the searing heat, the Beast's black and red scales glistened. It seemed Blaze couldn't remain a ghost in the midst of the smoking molten rock. The dragon hovered over Tom's shadow but the solid Beast was no danger to a silhouette.

"You've done it!" said Elenna. "Epos is free."

But Tom knew that this Beast Quest was far from over. He still couldn't move properly and was vulnerable until his shadow returned to him.

Tom called his shadow back but Blaze had already spotted him kneeling on the on the remains of the ice. The dragon turned his massive body, and began flying toward him. Tom's shadow ran behind, but it wasn't as quick as the Beast.

As Blaze slithered through the air toward him,

Tom saw the amulet piece near the dragon's shoulder again — the amulet piece he needed to bring his father back to his flesh-and-blood form. Now he feared that would never happen. The blue jaws gaped, ready to devour him.

CHAPTER TEN

FACE-TO-FACE WITH MALVEL

An arrow thudded into Blaze's neck. The Beast veered off course and smashed into the ground. The distraction gave Tom's shadow enough time to return to his body.

As Tom joined up with his shadow once more, power surged through him. He sprang to his feet. "Thanks, Elenna!" he called.

"Now finish that Beast!" she yelled back.

"With pleasure," Tom muttered, seeing Blaze rise up. No longer could he use his ghostly form to escape. Now the fight was fair.

Blaze's yellow eyes flashed. "You'll die in this

volcano, Tom," said a voice. It was a roar but the tone was Malvel's.

The ice dragon sent a jet of freezing air toward Tom. He threw himself out of the way, feeling the icy air brush his legs.

Epos swooped and crashed into Blaze, her talons raking his skin. Tom saw something drop to the ground and land in the corner of the volcano next to a bubbling chasm of lava.

The amulet fragment!

Blaze shook Epos loose.

"Get the amulet piece!" Tom shouted to Elenna, as Malvel's Beast faced him again. The dragon released another jet of ice and Tom charged forward, ducking beneath the freezing, icy stream and stabbing upward with his sword. The blade lodged in the thick scales of the dragon's stomach and Tom lost his grip on the hilt as Blaze soared up into the air.

Looking over, Tom saw Elenna slip the precious amulet fragment inside her pocket, and he ran to her side.

Blaze whipped around to face them and stalked forward, Tom's sword still hanging from his underside. Tom and Elenna found themselves right by the edge of a molten pool.

There was nowhere they could go.

Epos cawed from above and descended to attack Blaze, but the dragon flicked his tail out and sent the winged flame spinning into the lava.

"I told you that you'd die here," screeched Malvel's voice.

The ice dragon arched his back, and readied himself for the killing attack. But instead of fear, Tom felt a strange calm. There was a way out of this predicament. He just had to outsmart both the Beast and the Dark Wizard.

Tom took a few steps forward.

"What are you doing?" shouted Elenna. "You'll get yourself killed."

"Stay back!" said Tom. If Elenna was too close, his plan would fail.

White smoke appeared in Blaze's nostrils and the dragon opened his mouth to release his icy breath. Tom waited until the last possible moment and then lifted his shield as the blast shot forth. The freezing air hammered into his shield. Peering over the rim, Tom saw the flow of ice rebounding off the shield's surface and deflecting back at Blaze, encasing him in ice. Tom held on as the wood of his shield creaked. The air around him was bitterly cold, but Tartok's claw, which he'd won when he freed the ice beast, protected him.

Slowly a thick, icy barrier appeared between Tom and Blaze, and it reached all the way out to the edge of the volcano's wall.

Tom checked behind him and saw his friend

shivering with the cold. Her teeth were chattering, but she managed a smile. Tom was glad she'd stayed back; any closer, and her blood would have frozen in her veins.

She held a shaky arm out, and pointed past him. "M-M-Malvel," she stuttered.

Tom turned back and saw the Dark Wizard lying on the ground beside the frozen Beast. The cold must have driven him out of Blaze's body. He climbed to his feet, shaking his head in confusion before catching sight of Tom through the ice wall. He stepped forward and ran his fingers over the cold surface, his eyes never leaving Tom's.

"Blaze is finished," Tom told Malvel. "And so are you . . ."

The Dark Wizard smashed one fist against the wall. Then the other.

"This isn't over!" he screamed. "I'll have my revenge!"

Tom ran at the wall, hoping to smash through it. A thin crack appeared. He wanted nothing more than to face his arch enemy one-on-one.

But Malvel's mouth curled to a smirk, and he slowly backed away. "Another time, young adversary," he said. "Another time."

"While there's blood in my veins," shouted Tom, shouldering the ice again, "I'll defeat you!"

Malvel's form seemed to drift out the volcano wall, and Blaze faded away with him. The sword that had been in the dragon's belly clattered to the ground.

Epos appeared by their side, her wings blazing with healthy flames. A fireball hovered between her talons. Tom stepped back from the wall as the winged flame sent it spinning into the ice.

As the fire died, a hole appeared in the center, melting outward. When it was big enough, Tom and Elenna climbed through.

Tom knelt and picked up his sword. "Malvel

was so close to us," he said. "Almost close enough to touch."

"Don't worry, Tom," she said. "At least we have this." She held up the amulet piece.

Tom took it and joined it with the other amulet pieces that were around his neck. As soon as he did, a light appeared before them, almost blinding in its brightness. And there, only a few paces away, was a ghostly shape he knew as well as his own reflection.

"Father!" Tom cried.

"You have triumphed once more, my son," said Taladon. "Epos is safe, and Malvel is driven back for now."

Tom longed to throw his arms around his father, but he knew it was impossible. Until he collected the sixth and final piece of the amulet, his father would remain a ghost.

"We only have one more Quest to go," said Tom. "Then you'll be flesh and blood again."

Taladon nodded slowly. "One last Quest, but a Quest deadlier than all those that have come before. Hold fast your courage. You will need it."

With those words, he disappeared.

Tom longed to keep his father with him, but put his sadness from his mind.

The winged flame spread her wings. "I think she's offering us a ride," said Elenna.

Tom climbed onto the winged flame's back, and Elenna settled beside him. Epos leaped into the air, beat her wings, and took them up through the glowing crater. When they emerged into the clear air of Avantia, Tom heaved a sigh of relief. The frost from the land had gone.

They dismounted Epos on Stonewin's peak, and the winged flame dove back into the volcano.

Tom was pleased that he succeeded in this Quest but he knew that Malvel's sorcery would not be kept at bay for long. There was a sixth and final Beast to face.

"The end is close," Elenna said.

"One last push," he replied. *And I'll be ready when you come again, Malvel,* Tom thought. *I'll always be ready.*